My Brother Is a Visitor from Another Planet

To: Kevin Chipchase
From: Project STAR &
      Miss Conway
  Keep Reading!! :)

My Brother Is a Visitor from Another Planet

Dyan Sheldon

Illustrated by
Derek Brazell

CANDLEWICK PRESS
CAMBRIDGE, MASSACHUSETTS

First U.S. paperback edition 1995

Library of Congress Cataloging-in-Publication Data

Sheldon, Dyan.
    My brother is a visitor from another planet / Dyan Sheldon ;
illustrated by Derek Brazell.—1st U.S. ed.
    "First published in Great Britain by Viking Children's Books,
1992"—T.p. verso.
    Summary: Nine-year-old Adam's obnoxious older brother Keith
claims to be an alien from another galaxy and asks for Adam's help
because a spaceship is coming to take him back to his home planet.
    ISBN 1-56402-141-6 (hardcover)—ISBN 1-56402-517-9 (paperback)
    [1. Brothers—Fiction.   2. Extraterrestrial beings—Fiction.
3. Practical jokes—Fiction.]   I. Brazell, Derek, ill.   II. Title.
PZ7.S54144My   1993   [Fic]—dc20   92–53420

10 9 8 7 6 5 4 3 2 1

Printed in Great Britain

Candlewick Press
2067 Massachusetts Avenue
Cambridge, Massachusetts 02140

For Jack and Ryan

Chapter One

*F*or my ninth birthday, my parents gave me a bike. It was black with yellow trim. It had a light, a bell, a rack, and a pump. I said, "Wow! This is really wicked! This is the best present I've ever had."

My grandparents gave me a sweater. It had a football player, goalposts, and a football on it, because I really like football. I knew there was no way I could wear this sweater in public, you know, in front of other kids, but I smiled and tried to look happy anyway. My grandmother knit it herself. I said, "Thanks, Grandma. Thanks, Grandpa."

My brother gave me an old key ring. He gave it to me wrapped in leftover Christmas paper and two days late. This key ring used to have a picture of Bo Jackson on it, but the picture had disappeared. I think it happened the time he accidentally left the key ring in his jeans when they were being washed. I said, "Is this it, then? Is this my gift?" For his birthday, I'd given him this really awesome T-shirt. I'd had to save my allowance for about three years to buy it, but the Patriots is his favorite team. And Keith's my only brother. You want to give your only brother something really special when he turns thirteen, don't you?

Keith put a hand on my shoulder. "I'm really sorry, Adam," he said. "I really am truly sorry. I can't tell you how much it hurts me that I couldn't get you a real present." He held up his empty palms. "But I didn't have any money." He didn't sound really sorry. What he sounded was guilty. But he looked sorry. His eyes were all scrunched up and his mouth was turned down. My brother's good at that, looking sorry. My

dad says it's probably because Keith always has something to be sorry about. He gets a lot of practice.

I stared at the key chain in my hand. Not only had the picture dissolved in the laundry, but the plastic was scratched and there was a nick in one corner.

"Don't lie," I said. "If you had no money, it's because you spent it on yourself. You bought that new Walkman and then you didn't have anything left to spend on me." I know it doesn't matter how much something costs. I know it's the thought that counts. But I couldn't see that very much thought had gone into this.

"You don't understand," said my brother. "It was an absolute emergency." He was breaking my heart. "I had no choice, Adam. I *had* to buy it."

An emergency? The last time my brother had an emergency was when our parents were out and he and his friends ordered a pizza from around the corner. When the delivery man arrived, Keith discovered they didn't have enough money to pay for it. "It's an emergency," he told me. "I'll pay you back Friday." So I paid for the pizza. I paid for the pizza with the allowance I'd been saving, but he would only let me have one slice. I paid for the pizza, he only let me have one slice, *and* he never paid me back.

"Oh, right," I said. "I'll bet it was an emergency."

My brother shook his head sadly. The way he shook his head told me that I was being stupid. "Adam," he said, "Adam, I can explain this time. I really can." He shook his head sadly again. "You're going to feel really bad when you learn the truth. You're going to wish you'd been a whole lot nicer to me."

I folded my arms across my chest. I had heard this before, too. The last time Keith told me I was going to wish I'd been a whole lot nicer to him was when he wanted my new sleeping bag to go camping with. He told me he had only six months to live. He lost my sleeping bag in some river *and* he didn't die. He wasn't even sick. "So go ahead," I said. "Explain."

My brother looked around as if he thought we were being watched. He put a finger to his lips. He shook his head. We were in our room, sitting on his bed, and he was acting as if we were in a spy film. "Not here," he whispered. "It's not safe."

"What are you talking about?" I shouted. "We're in your room, Keith. Mom and Dad are in the living room. Elvis is right outside the door." Elvis is my dog. "What do you mean, it's not safe?"

He clamped a hand over my mouth. "Come on," he hissed. "Let's go up to the park and I'll tell you there."

Chapter Two

*I*t was just getting dark and there was a chill in the air. My brother pulled on his sweater and his knit cap. I put on my jacket and snapped Elvis's leash on his collar. Well, I tried to snap Elvis's leash on his collar. It always takes me a few minutes to put Elvis on his leash — he gets so excited when he knows he's going out that he won't stop jumping up and down.

"Hurry up, will you, Adam?" Keith grumbled. "I don't want to stand in the hallway for the next year and a half."

"Where are you boys off to?" called my mother from the living room. "I was just going to make some hot chocolate."

"We'll have some when we come back," said Keith. "We're taking the dog for a walk."

Elvis and I looked at each other. Keith had never taken Elvis for a walk in his life. The only thing he ever did to Elvis was torture him. He'd pretend to throw him his ball. He'd wave something Elvis really liked in front of Elvis's face — a barbecue potato chip or a chocolate cookie — and then he'd eat it himself. He'd stand up at the window and then hiss at Elvis, "Get the cat! Get the cat!" until Elvis went berserk barking and trying to scratch through the glass to get the cat. It didn't matter if there was a cat outside. Keith would also pretend to be the vacuum cleaner. He'd wait until Elvis was sleeping peacefully on the couch and then he'd charge into the living room going *vroom-vroom-vroom*.

"Oh, that's nice," said my mother. "Don't be too long, though." And then, just in case we hadn't noticed, she said, "It's getting dark."

"We won't be long," said my brother. He made a face at me. "At the rate Adam's going, we'll never leave."

"There," I said, trying to avoid Elvis's tongue. He gets very grateful when you take him out. "We're ready."

"It's about time," said Keith, and he punched me in the arm as we walked through the door.

My brother wouldn't talk to me till we got to the park. He said this was because he wanted to be at a place where he was sure no one could

13

overhear us. I said who did he think was going to overhear us on the street? It was practically time for supper. Everybody was either indoors or in their cars. My brother said that showed how little I understood. He said he envied me, being so young and innocent and everything.

When we got to the park, Keith said he couldn't feel safe until we were away from the crowds. "Crowds?" I said. "What crowds?" It was spring, and a few people were strolling along. And there were a lot of dog walkers. But it wasn't exactly like Star Market on a Saturday.

We crossed to a meadow and walked into the middle of it. There was no crowd out there. I let Elvis off his leash. Keith just stood there, staring up at the sky as though he were looking for something. There are always a lot of planes overhead because of the airport, and it was a cloudy night. When it's cloudy like that, all you can see of the planes are their lights cutting through the clouds. It makes them look sort of special. Like spaceships or something. When Keith and I were younger and still played together, we used to pretend that that was what they were: spaceships. I figured that was what he was looking for now, planes flying through the clouds.

I was just deciding that Keith was putting me on as usual and that I should go home by myself when he suddenly remembered I was there. He looked down at me. "Are you sure you really want to hear this?" he asked.

"Sure I'm sure."

"You're positive?"

Was I sure? Was I positive? Why did he always have to make such a big deal of everything? Why couldn't he just tell me?

"Yeah, Keith, I'm absolutely completely positive."

He sighed. "Okay," he said. "If you're really sure."

"Keith," I said, "I'm really sure."

He became silent. He stared at me for a few seconds. He jammed his hands in his pockets and sighed again. He looked up at the sky. He stared at the ground for a few seconds. And then he told me why he had spent the money he could have used to buy me a birthday present on something for himself: he had to.

"I didn't want to buy that new Walkman," he said. "I *had* to buy it." Even though the only other person there was a girl way at the other side of the field, walking one of those skinny little dogs that looks like a rat on a rope, he was whispering.

"You *had* to? Why? Because Mom and Dad gave you those speakers for your birthday?" They were really neat, these speakers. You hooked them

15

up to your Walkman and you didn't need the headphones.

"No, Adam," said my brother. "Because I really had to buy it." He was talking very slowly, as though I didn't understand English very well. "I told you. It was an emergency."

I kicked a rock across the grass, but I missed Keith. Elvis went running after it.

"Some emergency," I said. "You could have waited a week or two!" I kicked another rock. I hit Elvis. He ran off. "You could at least have bought me a new key chain."

My brother put his arm around my shoulder. "Adam," he whispered, "Adam, listen to me. You don't understand. You think I just wanted a new Walkman so I could listen to tapes."

Well, that was pretty stupid of me, wasn't it?

"No," I said. "No. I think you bought it so you can watch television on it."

He patted my shoulder. "Hey, Adam," he said, "you're not as dumb as you look. That's actually

not too far off." He leaned down so that his head was close to mine. "Adam," he whispered,

"Adam, what I needed it for was intergalactic communications."

Well, that was better. Intergalactic communications. That made sense.

Keith's voice was so soft that even though I could smell the Life Savers on his breath at first I wasn't sure that I had heard him right. "You what?" I said.

"Intergalactic communications," he repeated. "My old one was all worn out." He gave me another wink. "You know what intergalactic communications are, don't you?"

I shook his arm off me. "Of course I know."

Whenever Keith asks me if I know what something is, I automatically say yes. I guess it's a habit. I say yes when I know what he's talking about, and I say yes when I don't. If he asked me something in Greek, I'd probably say I understood him. I don't want him to think I'm stupid just because I'm younger than he is.

"Intergalactic communications," he repeated again. "You're sure you know?"

"Sure I'm sure."

Keith has dark, beady eyes, like a lizard's. They go right through you.

I stared at my feet. "It's communications between galactics." I made sure I mumbled. If you mumble, people think you said the right thing even if you didn't. It usually works with my mother, but not with my brother.

"Galaxies," he corrected. He stared up at the sky again. "Communications between galaxies." He can smile like a lizard, too.

I looked out across the meadow. The dog walker had gone home and there was no sign of Elvis. I turned up my collar — it was getting cold. "I knew that," I said. But of course what I knew was that I had no idea what he was talking about. Intergalactic communications? My brother couldn't even remember to phone home when he was late from school.

Something moved in the shadows. Keith put his hand over my mouth. "Shhh," he said. "What was that?" He looked to the left. He looked to the right.

"Let go," I ordered. "You're going to suffocate me." I tried to bite his hand.

He let go. But he held on to my jacket. "Adam," he hissed. "Adam, if I tell you my secret, will you give me your word that you'll never tell a living soul?"

"Sure," I said. "Of course I won't tell."

"Promise?" He got a headlock on me.

I winced, but I winced silently. "I promise."

He tightened his grip. "You've got to give me your solemn oath, Adam, on Elvis's life."

That sounded pretty serious. Usually Keith's secrets were about who broke Dad's electric razor, where he really was when my mother thought he was sleeping over at Charlie Donaldson's house, or some girl he had a crush on. But I never had to swear to secrecy on the life of my dog before. Maybe he was in trouble at school. Maybe some bully was threatening him. Or maybe this time he and Charlie really were going to run away and join a rock band.

"Ow," I said, "you're hurting me."

He leaned down so his mouth was almost in my ear. Cherry Life Savers and spit. "If you tell anyone, Adam, I won't be responsible for what happens to you or that mutt."

"Don't call him a mutt," I yelled back. "He's a South Street retriever." That's what my mother always tells people Elvis is because that was where she found him. He was sitting outside the train station with an injured foot.

Keith squeezed harder. "Promise, Adam. On the mutt's life."

He was really hurting me. I thought that maybe he'd broken my neck. It's hard not to cry when you think your brother's broken your neck, but I try not to cry in front of Keith unless I really can't help it. It never makes him stop doing what he's doing; it just makes him laugh or call me names.

"I promise, Keith," I said. "I won't tell anyone."

"Not even the Midget," said my brother.

The Midget's my best friend, Jerome. He's not really a midget, but he's not tall, either. My mother says he's the only nine-year-old she knows who wears out his clothes instead of growing out of them.

"Not even Midge." I gasped. "Let go, Keith."

"I just hope that I really can trust you," said my brother. He released me so quickly that I fell over. "Because I'm desperate, Adam. I need your help. I really and truly need your help."

I got to my feet. I dusted off my jeans. "Hey," I said, "of course you can trust me. What else are brothers for?"

Chapter Three

As it turned out, my brother wasn't in trouble at school, there weren't any tough kids threatening to turn him into hamburger, and he and Charlie weren't going to learn to play more than one song on the guitar and grow their hair long. It was just that my brother came from another planet. Another galaxy, to be precise. You'd think I would have guessed.

"Oh, right," I said. I was laughing pretty hard. "What do you think I am, Keith? Stupid or something?"

He just stood there, silently staring at me with his lizard eyes like I was stupid or something.

"Right," I said. "You expect me to believe that you come from another planet?" I'd always known Keith was weird, but there's weird and there's weird.

"Another galaxy," corrected my brother.

In the nine years I had known him, my brother had told me a lot of things that I believed and that I shouldn't have believed. I mean besides that he had six months to live. He told me he saw the Loch Ness monster in the Charles River. He told me he met Bo Jackson at the deli. He told me Mr. Meeker, the man next door, was a vampire. He told me my parents had found me in the supermarket, right next to the melons. If you want to feel really stupid sometime, try asking your mother if she was ever sorry she took you instead of a cantaloupe.

After all those dumb stories, there was no way I was going to fall for this one. Not in a million years. I lifted my left leg. "Go on," I said, "pull the other one."

But Keith just stood there with his hands in his pockets. "It's not a joke," he said. "This time I'm really telling you the truth."

"Oh, sure you are," I said. It was so quiet out in the meadow that my voice sounded loud. "Sure. Just like you were when you told me the Loch Ness monster was purple and ate hamburgers."

Keith put a hand on my shoulder. "Adam," he said quietly. "Adam, let's not forget about where paper comes from, all right?"

The only time I hadn't believed Keith when I should have was the time he told me paper was made from trees. I thought it was the funniest thing I'd ever heard in my life. "Paper from trees?" I screamed. "Paper from trees?" I rolled on the carpet. I kicked my legs on the floor. I was laughing so hard that I choked. My mother came rushing in because she thought Keith must be trying to kill me again. "You know what he said?" I laughed. "He said paper is made from trees! Can you imagine? Paper from trees!" My mother just stood there giving me a very serious look. It was the same look she'd given me when I had asked about the cantaloupe.

But I was wise to Keith's tricks. That was the way he always talked me into things. He made me feel dumb. He made me doubt myself. He said things like, "You mean you've never noticed that Mr. Meeker sleeps all day, Adam? Gee, how could you miss that?" He scratched his head. He looked puzzled. He said, "You mean you never noticed that Mr. Meeker doesn't leave the house until it's dark?" He laughed until he couldn't breathe. "Oh boy," he said, "I bet you thought Mr. Meeker worked nights or something."

But this time he wasn't going to trick me into anything. This time it wasn't going to work.

"This is different," I argued. Even I could see that. "If you think about it, it makes sense that paper comes from trees." We'd had a lot of rain recently, and the ground was soft. I dug my toe into the earth. "But it doesn't make sense that you're from another planet."

"What do you mean it doesn't make sense?" asked my brother. "You don't think I could really be related to *you*, do you?"

Ha-ha-ha, so funny I forgot to laugh. I dug deeper.

He stopped laughing. "Really, Adam," he said. "I can prove it. Beyond any reasonable doubt."

I pulled my foot out of the ground. I couldn't see it, but I could feel the mud squelching into my sneaker. My mother was going to murder me. "So prove it," I said.

My brother stuck his hands back in his pockets and started walking away. "Tonight," he said.

My brother walked home in front of me and Elvis. He was whistling under his breath, and every once in a while he'd stop all of a sudden and look up at the sky.

Boy, I thought, he must think I'm about as smart as a turkey if he believes I'm going to swallow this one. Mrs. Vorha, my teacher, had told us all about turkeys. Turkeys are so stupid that they drown in the rain. They lean their heads back to see what's happening, they open their mouths, and they drown.

"Can you believe it?" I said to Elvis, loud enough so my brother would hear me. "He thinks if he looks up at the stars, I'll think he's E.T."

But my brother didn't start arguing or defending himself, like he usually did. He didn't say anything. He just kept walking ahead of us, whistling. It wasn't like him at all. And I could tell he was smiling to himself. It drove me nuts.

And I'll tell you what else drove me nuts. Usually, if my brother told me something I wasn't supposed to tell anyone, he would stop under the

front light when we got home, shove me against the wall, and threaten me to make sure I didn't talk. But not this time. This time he just opened the door and walked inside and let it bang shut behind him, as though Elvis and I weren't even there.

And usually, if my brother and I had some secret together, he would spend the evening giving me special looks or discussing it in whispers. But not this time. We set the table together and the only thing he said to me was, "We're short one fork." We washed our hands for supper together and the only time he looked at me was when I dropped the soap.

But the thing that drove me really nuts was that Keith's weird behavior meant I couldn't completely convince myself he was putting me on. I don't know why, but there was this dumb little voice in my head that kept saying, "What if he isn't putting you on, Adam? What if he really is from another planet? What then?"

"Don't be crazy," I'd answer this little voice. "It's impossible. This isn't *Star Trek*, it's Chestnut Drive."

"Impossible?" asked the little voice. It sounded a lot like Keith. "Think about it, Adam. Is it really impossible?"

So I thought about it. Maybe it wasn't impossible. I mean, it could happen, couldn't it? You know, in theory. It happened in movies and books and stuff like that. And my grandpa's always talking about how things have changed in the last fifty years. You know, how when he was a boy they'd only just invented the typewriter and now everybody was using computers. How when he was young the automobile was like a miracle, and now men had walked on the moon. "Yesterday's science fiction is today's reality," my grandpa always says.

"You see?" said this little voice. "It's not impossible after all, is it?"

My teacher, Mrs. Vorha, says that logic is the enemy of ignorance. "Don't be a silly goat," Mrs. Vorha always says. "Be logical. Be smart."

So I decided to be smart. I decided to ignore the little voice and use logic.

First of all, logic said, my brother couldn't really be from another galaxy because my parents would have told me. Having a close relative from outer space had to be something like being adopted. If you're adopted, your parents have to tell you when you reach a certain age. Midge is adopted, and his parents told him when he was seven. So if Keith really was from another planet, Mom and Dad would have taken me aside for a little talk. "Son," they would have said, "we have something to tell you. Your brother isn't really your brother. He's really a spaceship captain from Alpha Centauri."

The second thing logic said was that if Keith wasn't really a Wiggins, I would have noticed. I mean, how could I not have noticed? We lived in the same house. We shared a bedroom. We ate together. We dressed together. We brushed our teeth together. We'd followed Mr. Meeker together. Sometimes, after we watched a really scary horror movie, we even slept together. You can't share a bedroom with someone and not notice that he spends a lot of his spare time communicating intergalactically. You can't sleep in the same bed with someone and not notice that he doesn't have a pulse.

That night we had spaghetti with meatballs and leftover birthday cake for supper. Spaghetti with meatballs and leftover birthday cake are two of my favorite things in the world, but I was too busy using logic to eat.

Why would someone from another galaxy want to live with Mom and Dad and me? It's not like we're famous. It's not even like my parents are scientists or something and know all these government secrets. My dad makes the best chocolate cake in Boston, and my mom's spaghetti with meatballs is awesome, but you wouldn't travel across the universe for that, would you? Not even Keith would do that. I had to be right. He was putting me on.

"What's the matter, Adam?" asked my Dad. "Don't you feel well?"

I was twirling the spaghetti onto my fork and then untwirling it again — twirling and untwirling, twirling and untwirling. "No," I said, "I feel fine."

"You're not still sulking because I yelled at you about your sneakers, are you?" asked my mother. She turned to my father. "You should have seen the state they were in," she told him. "*And* his socks!" She shook her head. "Sometimes I don't think either of them has the sense he was born with."

My father just went on eating, so I guess he agreed with her.

Keith looked up from shoveling spaghetti into his mouth. "Hey, don't lump me together with Adam," he protested. "We're nothing alike." He gave me a wink.

Chapter Four

*M*y brother came tiptoeing into our room from the bathroom. He shut the door really quietly and then put his ear to it, listening. Satisfied that he wasn't being followed, he locked the door. He turned on the light on his dresser and switched off the overhead. At last he looked at me. "Okay," he said, "are you ready for this?"

"I'm ready," I said.

If you want to know the truth, I'd been ready for hours. Right after supper I'd excused myself and gone into our room to wait for Keith, but Keith hadn't come. There I was, sitting by myself on my bed, feeling like a complete jerk, while he was sitting in the living room with Mom and Dad, watching TV. It was one of my favorite shows, too. Every once in a while I'd hear him laugh. It drove me up the wall.

But now Mom and Dad had sent him to bed, and here was Keith, rolling up one leg of his pajamas. He pointed to the back of his knee. "Look," he said. "Look there, where my finger is."

I looked.

"What do you see?" asked my brother.

"The back of your knee."

Keith groaned. "How can you be so stupid?"

I started to say that I wasn't stupid, but he cut me off.

"Look closer," he ordered. "Try using your eyes."

I looked closer. "I don't see anything," I said.

"What? Are you blind?" he hissed. "Look where I'm pointing, Adam! Not at the floor!"

I looked again. There was something there. Or was there? I squinted. Yes, I saw something there. Something very, very small. Right at the crack at the back of his knee were two tiny scars.

"Do you see it?" asked Keith.

"You mean the thing that looks like a snakebite?"

"Yeah, the thing that looks like a snakebite," he mimicked.

"So what?" I said. This was what I'd waited around all night for? Two pinpricks at the back of his knee?

"So what?" mimicked Keith. He dropped his pajama leg and turned around. "Where have you been, Adam? Locked in the nursery?"

I was getting annoyed. "I've been right here, waiting for you," I snapped. "That's where I've been."

Keith rolled his eyes. "What do you think those marks mean?" He shook his head. "What do you think? That they're there for no reason? Don't you know *anything* about extraterrestrials, Adam?" He sounded really concerned.

Logic started to desert me. "Sure I do," I shot

back. "Only they're all different, aren't they, Keith? It depends what planet you're from, you know."

Keith smiled. He leaned forward so that his face was close to mine. "Well, on my planet," he said in a heavy whisper, "you have to be vaccinated before you can come to Earth. And that's what those two little scars are, Adam. They're my vaccination."

Logic returned. "You mean like for smallpox?"

Keith thought that was hysterical. "You Earthlings," he gasped. "You really make me laugh!"

"And you make me laugh," I said. I laughed. "Ha-ha-ha." I started to get into bed. "That's not proof, Keith," I said. I punched my pillow into shape. "Two tiny scars? What kind of proof is that?"

"It's not the only proof I have," said Keith.

"Oh, sure," I said. "You probably have a scratch on your arm that shows you're a starship commander or something." I reached up and snapped off the light over my bed.

"No, really Adam," said my brother. "Watch this. Here's something humans can't do."

I looked over, trying not to appear too interested. "What?" I asked. "Don't tell me you can make your eyes glow in the dark."

"Not in your planet's atmosphere, I can't,"

said my brother. "But I can do something just as good." He was standing beside his bed, staring at the light on his dresser. "Watch this, Adam," he said in a flat voice.

He lifted his hand and pointed a finger at the lamp on his dresser. It had a green shade and the base was a golden retriever. The bulb fitted into the top of the retriever's head.

"Now what?" I giggled. "That's the lamp Grandpa made for you two Christmases ago."

"*Shhh*," hissed my brother. "Just watch."

I watched. My brother flicked his finger. The lamp went out.

"Now I'm going to move my finger again and turn it back on," Keith announced. He wasn't even finished talking when the light came back on.

He was smiling. "Believe me now?"

Logic said that it was impossible to turn off a lamp that looked like a golden retriever just by looking at it. In fact, because my grandfather had done something wrong when he put in the socket, it was hard to turn the lamp off by hand.

"Do it again," I ordered.

Keith did it again. "Not only that, Adam, but I can read minds."

Now that was really funny. "Oh, sure," I said. "Keith, you can just about read the back of a cereal box."

"It's true, Adam. You'd be surprised at the things I know about you that you don't think I know."

It was a frightening thought. "Like what?"

My brother smiled. "Like where you've hidden your birthday money."

I laughed with relief. He couldn't know that. I changed the hiding place twice a day, just to be safe. That morning I'd hidden it in the toe of my boot, and this afternoon I'd taped it to the

back of my desk.

My brother closed his eyes. "Let me concentrate," he said. "Yes, I see it. It's in the toe of your left boot at the back of your closet."

I was a little surprised that he'd gotten that right. But it didn't really matter, of course, because he was still wrong. Only before I could tell him that, he said, "No, wait a minute. It *was* in your boot. Now it's taped to the back of your desk." He opened his eyes. "Well?" If he smiled any more his face would split in two.

But I was holding on to logic now. I wasn't going to let it desert me again. Not without a fight. I became inspired. "What about your birth certificate?" I asked. "I've seen it, Keith. Mom keeps it in her desk."

He made a face. "What do you think we are, dummies?" asked my brother. "I belong to a superior life form, Adam. Of course I have a birth certificate. We've thought of everything."

Logic was trying to wiggle away, but I kept a grip. "What about Mom?" I asked. "Mom would've told me if you weren't really my brother."

He made another face. "Adam," said my brother, "Mom doesn't know."

"Mom doesn't know?"

"Of course not," said Keith.

I couldn't accept this. My mom knew everything. If you ripped your jeans and tried to hide them at the bottom of your dresser, my mom knew. If you ate a few more cookies than you were supposed to, my mom knew. If you didn't really have a headache but wanted to stay home and watch TV, my mom knew. How could we have an alien being living at 33 Chestnut Drive and my mom not know? "Mom must know," I protested. "She must."

Keith shook his head. "She doesn't know, Adam. No one knows but you. And the only reason you know is because I need your help."

"*You* need *my* help?" Well, that was a change. I was usually the one who needed his help. And he was usually the one who wouldn't give it to me. "What for?"

My brother sat down on my bed. "It's like this," he said. "My mission here is completed."

I couldn't help interrupting. "Your mission?" I asked. My brother never even finished his chores. He expected me to believe he'd completed a mission? "And what was that?"

"I can't tell you," said Keith. "It's top secret. The important thing is that it's finished and now I'm supposed to return home."

He really did think I was dumb. I stayed cool. "So?" And then a pretty pleasant thought occurred to me. If Keith was telling the truth and he really did return to his planet, then I'd be an only child — an only child with his own room.

Keith shook his head sadly. "So I don't want to go." He gestured toward our room. "I like it here, Adam. My home planet's pretty boring compared to here. We don't have football. We don't have television. We don't have barbecue potato chips."

No football? No chips? And they were supposed to be superior to us? "What about hamburgers and ice cream?"

"We don't even have chocolate cookies."

I tried not to look too disappointed. It figured that when I finally had a chance to get rid of my brother he wouldn't budge. "I don't see what the

40

problem is," I said once I'd gotten over this news. "Can't you just tell them you don't want to go?"

He shook his head again. "That's why I had to buy the Walkman, Adam. The communicator I brought with me broke and I lost contact with my ship. They're coming for me on Friday, and I haven't been able to tell them I'm not going to leave." He lowered his voice. "They'll be really

angry if they find out at the last minute," he said.

They sounded a little like Mom. "So what do you want me to do?" I asked cautiously. Knowing Keith, it wouldn't have surprised me if he wanted me to go in his place.

"It's easy." He smiled. He patted my knee. "I've rigged up another communicator, but it's not very powerful. I need to boost my transmission."

Boost his transmission? What was he talking about now?

"You understand what I mean, don't you Adam?" asked my brother.

"Oh, sure," I said. "Boost your transmission. I know what you mean."

"Good." He patted my knee again. "That's where you come in. I need you to operate the auxiliary antenna."

Boost his transmission. Auxiliary antenna. I had no idea what he meant, but it sounded real. It wasn't the kind of thing you'd make up. Not even Keith would make it up.

"The auxiliary antenna, Adam. You know, to give me more power — to boost my transmission?"

I nodded. "I know, Keith. So you get better reception."

Keith smiled. "Do you think you can handle

that, Adam?"

"Sure," I said. "Sure I can handle that." I sort of wished I had some idea what it was he wanted me to do.

"Good," said my brother. "You're a real pal." He got up and went over to his bed. he pointed a finger at the golden retriever lamp and it went off. I heard him settle under the blankets.

"Keith?" I whispered into the dark.

"What?" he mumbled. He was half asleep.

"Keith, if it isn't like a smallpox vaccination, what is it for?"

He rolled toward the wall. "It's to make me look human," said my brother. "Good night, Adam."

"'Night, Keith."

Chapter Five

"You look a little pale this morning, Adam," said my mother. "Are you feeling all right?"

I ducked behind the cereal box. "Yeah," I answered, "I'm fine."

I felt awful. I'd slept really badly. Elvis came over and put his chin on my knee. He felt pretty awful too. He'd slept badly because my tossing and turning kept waking him up.

All night long I'd dreamed about my brother. It was one of those dreams that never end. Every time you think it's going to end, it starts over again.

In my dream, I was running down a dark tunnel, and Keith was running after me. He was laughing. "You want to see what I *really* look like?" he was shouting. "Adam! Wait up! Don't you want to see the *real* me?" I'd be running and running, way ahead of him, and then for some dumb reason I'd suddenly stop and turn around. It happened over and over again. One time when I turned around, he looked like an upright iguana. And I can remember thinking in my dream, *I don't believe this! The brother I let drink out of the glass I drink from is really a reptile from Mars!* Another time he was smooth and rubbery, with big yellow eyes. And another time his brain was outside his head and he had an extra arm. It was really gross. That was when I kicked Elvis off the bed.

"You seem very quiet," said my mother.

My mother would have made an excellent policewoman. "It's early, Mom," I said, shaking some cornflakes into my bowl. "I'm not awake yet."

"Have some juice," said my mother, handing me a glass. "That should do the trick."

Just then Keith charged into the room. He already had his jacket on and his books in his arms.

My mother gave him one of her looks. "Keith Wiggins," said my mother, "just where do you think you're going? You haven't had your breakfast yet!"

I couldn't help feeling a little sorry for her, talking to Keith as though he were perfectly normal. She thought Keith had her eyes and nose, but for all we really knew he had three heads and a tail. Usually my mother threw a fit when she found out that instead of changing your socks every day, like she told you to, you sometimes wore them two days in a row. She'd be very upset if she ever learned the truth about Keith.

"I don't have time, Mom," said Keith. "I have to meet Charlie. I'm already late."

"Keith," said my mother. "You can't go out on an empty stomach."

I wished she'd stop being so motherly to him. My poor mom! What if the truth did get out? She'd never be able to go to the corner store again. "Ooh, there's Mrs. Wiggins," everybody would whisper. "One of her sons looks like E.T."

Keith picked up my juice and drank half of it in one long swallow. "There," he said. "Now I have to go." He turned at the door. "See you later, Adam," he said, smiling. He gave me a wink and blew my mother a kiss.

Suddenly, all I wanted to do was be on my bike, pedaling as fast as I could. I didn't think I could stay in the house for another second knowing what I knew, that my mother was being sent kisses by a creature from outer space. I got up so fast Elvis banged his head on the table. "I'd better get going too, Mom," I said. "Midge and I are supposed to ride to school together."

She folded her arms across her chest and frowned. "Aren't you at least going to finish your juice?" She made it sound like a question, but it was more a command.

I stared at the glass of juice. I couldn't do it. Alien lips had touched its rim. "I'm not really thirsty, Mom," I said. I grabbed my things and raced out the back door before she could say anything else.

But I couldn't concentrate on school. All I could think about was Keith. What was this mission of his? What did he really look like? Who were They? What if They wouldn't let him stay with my parents and me? What if They came and dragged him out of the house in front of everybody? I could just see all the neighbors peeking from behind

their blinds as all these guys straight out of *Star Wars* dragged my brother out of the house. Never mind not being able to go into the corner store anymore; my mother would never be able to go out on the street in daylight again.

"Adam," said Mrs. Vorha. "Adam, the class is waiting."

I looked around. She was right, the class was waiting. Everyone had turned around to stare at me. I wished I knew why. I glanced over at Midge. I could tell from the way he looked, like he was choking, that he was trying to think me the question Mrs. Vorha had asked. It wasn't working.

Mrs. Vorha tapped her toe. "Adam," said Mrs. Vorha, "are you intending to keep us all in suspense? Or could it be that you weren't paying attention again?"

The first time Mrs. Vorha had caught me not paying attention that morning was during our math lesson. Mrs. Vorha had asked me what seven times nine was, only I hadn't heard her because I'd just noticed something that really upset me. Sammy, the class salamander, had come to the side of his fish tank and was staring at me. Sammy had big yellow eyes and smooth, rubbery skin. Just like Keith had had in my dream! So when Mrs. Vorha said, "Who can tell me what seven

times nine is? Adam?" I didn't answer, "Fifty-six Mrs. Vorha," the way I should have. Instead, I sort of shouted, "Keith!"

I fixed my eyes on the stain on the wall just above Mrs. Vorha's head. "It could be that I wasn't paying attention again," I mumbled.

"I think that's exactly right," said Mrs. Vorha. "And I think you'd better start paying attention right now. Do you agree with me, Adam?"

But already I wasn't paying attention, because the stain on the wall was changing shape. For months it had been just a rusty-colored blob.

But now I could see that it was really a galaxy. A galaxy light-years away and in deepest space.

"Adam!" Mrs. Vorha was practically screaming. "Do you agree with me?"

I jumped.

Midge yelled, "Yes! Yes, he agrees!"

It was Monday, and every Monday after school Midge and I went to his place. It was our routine. Mondays we went to his house; Tuesdays we went to my house; Wednesdays, Thursdays, and Fridays we played football in the park. If we didn't play football on Wednesdays, we'd go to Midge's house. If we didn't play on Thursdays, we'd go to mine. Etcetera. It wasn't anything we'd ever sat down and planned, it was just how it worked.

"Do you want to stop at Pinky's on the way home?" asked Midge when we left school. Pinky's was a newsstand near his house. It had the best selection of comics and candy in the neighborhood.

"Sure," I said. "We could get some gummy worms, and the new *Mad* should be in." To tell the truth, I was looking forward to going to Midge's. Thinking about my brother all day was starting to make me feel crazy. One minute I'd tell myself, "You're nuts, Adam, Keith's putting you on." And the next minute I'd see that light going on and off and those two tiny, perfect dots at the back of his leg and I'd hear Grandpa saying, "Yesterday's science fiction is today's reality." Just saying "*Mad*" and "gummy worms" had made me feel normal again.

We reached the rack and started to unlock our bikes. "Adam," said Midge. He was starting to laugh. "Adam, why did you shout 'Keith!' like that when Mrs. Vorha asked you what seven times nine was?"

We started to wheel our bikes out of the yard. I looked at Midge and his laughing made me want to laugh too. "Man." I giggled. "Did you see her face?"

Midge nearly let go of his bike. "She hasn't looked that surprised since Lucinda Moon threw up in the poster paint during art."

He cracked me up. I slapped him on the shoulder. I wished that I hadn't given Keith my word that I wouldn't tell Midge. I really did.

Midge was smiling at me. "So," he said, "why did you?"

I knew that if I could just tell Midge, everything would be all right. I looked straight ahead so I could think clearly. It wasn't that Midge would tell anyone else. Midge always kept his word. He was completely trustworthy. The words "Midge, can you keep a secret?" were just on the tip of my tongue when I saw something up ahead that made me freeze. Midge kept wheeling his bike toward

the gate, but I stood still. There, standing right at the entrance to the school yard, was my brother. My brother *never* met me at school. Not even when he was supposed to. One time he was supposed to pick me up after school to go to the dentist, and I stood there for an hour and a half before the principal found me and drove me home.

"Hey," said Midge. "There's your brother!"

How could I have forgotten that Keith could read my thoughts? My body started to move again. "Yeah," I said, steaming past him. "I have to go, Midge. I'll see you tomorrow."

"It's Monday!" Midge shouted after me. "I thought you were coming to my house!"

But I was already at the gate.

"Adam!" Midge yelled. "Adam!"

"I hope you didn't say anything to Midge," Keith was saying as I ran up to him.

I had to catch my breath. "Of course not," I said. "I promised, didn't I?"

He put an arm around my shoulder. "That's right, Adam, you did promise." He smiled. "You promised on Elvis's life."

I could hear Midge right behind us. I didn't even turn around.

Chapter Six

Keith rode my bike home and I sat on the bar. I hate riding with Keith because he always tries to scare me. He'll pretend he's lost control and that we're going to hit a parked car. Or he'll make the bike wobble like we're going to fall. And he always rides too fast. Even when he's not in a hurry. Which, today, he was.

"Do you think you could go just a little slower?" I shouted as we went racing down Hillview Road. There wasn't a view anymore, just rows of houses, but the hill was still there.

"You don't have to be scared." Keith laughed. "You're with me!" He bucked the bike over the curb. "If we're about to hit something, I'll just make it fly!"

We took the corner so fast I thought we were flying. "I don't want to fly, Keith," I shouted. "I just want to get home in one piece."

"Me too," Keith shouted back. "Me too. Before Mom gets back."

That was why we were in such a hurry. On Mondays, Mom took Mrs. Pitelli, who lived behind us, to the doctor. Mrs. Pitelli is about a hundred years old and can't get there on her own. It meant that we would have the house to ourselves for about fifteen minutes. Thirty, if Mom took Mrs. Pitelli out for a cup of coffee on the way home. Fifteen minutes was just long enough for Keith to show me how to work the auxiliary antenna. And he had to show me today because he'd made a mistake. His spaceship wasn't coming for him on Friday, as he'd thought. It was coming on Wednesday. If he was going to contact them before they landed, he'd have to do it tomorrow.

We sort of stopped when we hit the front yard. "Quick!" Keith shouted. "Into the house!"

Keith closed the door of our room behind him. Although it was still daytime, he said, "I think we'll need a little light for this." He pointed a finger and turned on the golden retriever. It was beginning to seem like the normal way to turn on a lamp.

"Sit on your bed, Adam," he ordered. "We don't have much time."

I sat on my bed. After the ride we'd just had, I was happy to sit. My heart was pounding, and I wasn't even the one who had done all that pedaling. "Okay," I said. "I'm sitting."

Keith opened his closet door and took out his old black backpack. "Now I want you to pay very close attention to everything I say," he said. "You understand?"

"Of course I understand," I said, but I was looking around. I thought I could hear something humming softly, but I wasn't sure where the sound was coming from.

"Adam," snapped Keith. "I said close

56

attention." He sat down on his bed, facing me.

Was it coming from his side of the room? Or was it coming from right near me?

"Adam," said Keith. "If you're not going to do what I say —"

"Don't you hear it?" I asked. One second I was sure I could hear it and the next second I wasn't.

"It's just the electricity generated by my equipment," said Keith. "You're going to have to get used to it if you want to help me." He pointed to the bag. "Now I'm going to remove the antenna and show you what I mean." He lifted a silver box from the backpack. There were two wires coming out of one side. The lamp on his dresser began to blink. "It's very powerful," said Keith. "You have to be careful." I was sure the humming was getting a little louder. It was definitely coming from across the room. My brother stood up. "Here," he said, "you take it," and he handed me the silver box. The humming was louder now, but it wasn't coming from across the room, it was coming from right near me. I wasn't sure if it was behind me or under me, but I couldn't look because I was too busy staring at the auxiliary antenna.

I couldn't believe what I was holding in my

hand. I looked up at my brother. "Keith," I said, "this is your old Walkman."

"Adam," said my brother, "I know it's my old Walkman." He stretched out on his bed. "Do you think I came here with an auxiliary antenna? Do you think I *knew* my communicator was going to break? Is that what you think? I know I'm telepathic and have superior intelligence, Adam, but I can't foresee everything. I've had to make do."

The humming stopped.

I turned the player over in my hand. It was empty. I pulled back the cover over the batteries. It didn't have any batteries. All it had was the two wires where the headphones should have been. "Well, what am I supposed to do with it?" I asked.

"Turn it on," said my brother.

"I can't turn it on, Keith," I pointed out. "It doesn't have a tape in it."

"Turn it on anyway," said my brother.

"Keith!" He could really drive me crazy sometimes. "It doesn't have batteries!"

He jumped to his feet again. "Okay!" he shouted. "That's it. I'll do this without your help. Thank you very much!"

He reached for the Walkman, but I held on to it. "All I said was it doesn't have any batteries,

Keith. That's all I said. You don't have to get so upset."

He sat back down. "Yes I do," said my brother. He was calm again. "I have to, Adam, because I need you to do exactly what I say." He pointed at me. "Now turn on the antenna."

"Okay," I said. "Okay. I'm turning it on." I pushed Play.

My finger had hardly touched the button when suddenly the room was filled with static. You know, like when the radio isn't tuned right. I hate that sound. And this was really awful. It was really awful, because it was coming from right beside me *and* from across the room. Stereo static! I dropped the Walkman on the bed and just stared at it. The golden retriever was still blinking and there was all this noise coming from everywhere. I didn't know what to do. Part of me was really excited, and the other part of me wanted to run into the closet and hide.

The front door opened.

"Quick!" hissed my brother. "Turn it off! Mom's back!"

The noise stopped. The light stopped blinking.

"Keith!" called my mother. "Keith! Are you home?"

He grabbed the antenna off the bed. "At least we know it works," he whispered. He dropped it into his backpack and stuffed it under my bed just as my mother opened the bedroom door.

"Why, Adam!" said my mother. "What are you doing here? You're supposed to be at Jerome's."

Mom looked from me to Keith and from Keith to me. She was suspicious. She wasn't sure what she was suspicious of, but she was definitely suspicious. She really would have made an excellent detective. She probably would have ended up working at the seventh precinct. Detective Caroline Wiggins.

Keith and I both smiled at her. "Hi, Mom," we said. What else could we say?

Chapter Seven

Midge handed me half of his tuna sandwich and I handed him half of my peanut butter and jelly. We always swapped stuff from our packed lunches. It made life more interesting.

Midge lifted the top from the half I'd given him to make sure that my mother hadn't put any margarine on it. Midge hates peanut butter sandwiches with margarine, which is the way his mother makes them. My mother never makes them with margarine, but he likes to check anyway. He's that type of person.

"So where did you and Keith go yesterday?" asked Midge. Satisfied that my mom hadn't gone crazy with the margarine, he put the top back on.

I suppose it should have occurred to me that he might ask that question, but it hadn't. I'd had a lot of other things on my mind. I picked up my sandwich. "What?"

"Where did you and Keith go?"

I experienced a moment of panic. Where had we gone? I said the first thing that came to my mind. "Shopping," I said quickly. I took a big bite of tuna. Midge watched me. I chewed slowly.

"Shopping?" asked Midge. He was giving me a funny look. He knows I hate shopping.

I could see he wasn't going to give up on this until he had the answer he wanted. He's that type of person, too. The answer Midge wanted would explain why I hadn't told him I was going shopping. It would also explain why I hadn't asked him to come along.

"I completely forgot Keith was meeting me," I said, which was half true. "We had to get something for my dad's birthday." That was also half true. My dad did have a birthday. In January. In my mind I completed the sentence. *It's my dad's birthday in January*, I said in my mind. But out loud the next thing I said was, "This tuna's really good. What's your mom put in it? Hard-boiled egg?"

But Midge is not the kind of person who is interested in his mother's recipe for tuna sandwiches. "Your dad's birthday?" he repeated.

"Uh-huh. We thought we'd get him something together. You know, so we could buy something special."

"That makes sense," said Midge. But he was still giving me a funny look.

I decided to change the subject. "So," I said, "did you get *Mad?*"

Midge shook his head. "I thought we'd get it today, on the way to your house."

"Today?" I repeated.

"Yeah," said Midge. "Today. Today is

64

Tuesday, Adam. The day we always go to your house." He held out his bag of chips.

It was Tuesday, all right. But it wasn't the day we went to my house. It was the day I went to the park by myself. Because at exactly 3:35 I was to be on top of the hill near the duck pond. And at exactly 3:36 I was to turn on the auxiliary antenna. Keith would be at the other side of the park with his communicator, calling his ship.

Instead of taking a chip, I slapped my forehead. "Oh, gosh, Midge," I said. "Did I forget to tell you? I'm not going to be able to make it this afternoon, either."

Midge pulled the bag of chips out of my reach. "You're not?"

"I'm really sorry, Midge," I said. And I was really sorry.

"What are you doing instead?" asked Midge.

My mother says that I have a wild imagination. "Really, Adam," my mother always says, "I don't know where you get that wild imagination of yours. It certainly doesn't come from my family." But today my imagination wasn't wild at all. It was pretty boring. "Shopping," I said.

"Again?" asked Midge.

If my mother and Midge got together, they could probably start their own police force.

"Yeah," I said. I was thinking as fast as I could.

"We couldn't find anything yesterday." It wasn't great, but it made sense. "So we have to go back today."

Midge took a bite of his apple. "You want me to come along?"

A piece of tuna went down the wrong way. I started to choke. Midge slapped me on the back. A little harder than he had to, if you ask me.

"Well, gee," I said, when I'd recovered. "That'd be great, Midge. I mean, I'd love you to come, but you know what Keith's like."

Midge had known Keith almost as long as I had. Which meant that Keith treated Midge pretty much the way he treated me. Badly.

"Yeah," said Midge, "I know what he's like."

As soon as Mrs. Vorha dismissed us, I got all my things and headed for the door. Midge was right beside me. We walked to the bike rack together. We unlocked our bikes together. Side by side, we started walking toward the gate. I couldn't get rid of him.

"So," said Midge as we neared the street. "Where's your brother?"

"Oh, I'm not meeting him here," I said quickly. I looked at Midge. He didn't even have to ask the questions anymore. I answered them anyway. "We're meeting in front of Smith's."

"In front of Smith's?" said Midge. He pushed his glasses back on his nose. "That's not out of my way. I'll ride with you."

I got on my bike. "Smith's?" I repeated. "Did I say Smith's? I didn't mean Smith's, Midge. Smith's is where we went yesterday. I meant Collier's." Not only was Collier's in the direction of the park, it was also about three million miles from Midge's and all uphill. Midge didn't like riding uphill. Not with his little legs. I made a show of looking at my watch. "Oh, wow! Will you look at the time? I'm going to be late." I gave myself a push to get started. "See you tomorrow, Midge!" I called, and I tore down the road like I was being chased. I could feel him watching me the whole way.

I reached the park in record time. There were quite a few people around, walking their dogs and stuff like that. At the pond several mothers with little kids were feeding the ducks. It's strange how people like to feed ducks, but if you throw a couple of crumbs to a pigeon, everyone goes nuts. I got off my bike. No one paid any attention to me.

I walked my bike up the hill and parked it in the bushes. Then I parked myself in the bushes, too.

I found a good-sized rock to sit on, and I took the antenna out of my book bag. I held it in my hand. It was funny, but the antenna looked different out here from the way it had in our room. Yesterday, with the lamp flashing on and off and all that weird noise, it had really looked like something from a spaceship. But out here, with all the kids screaming and dogs barking and ducks quacking, it looked like a Walkman with no tape or batteries in it.

I checked my watch. Three thirty-one. Keith had made me synchronize my watch with his four times before I'd left the house that morning. "If you're a second off, Adam," he warned me, "you'll ruin the whole thing."

I looked up at the sky. There were some clouds, but otherwise it was empty. Flat, blue, and empty. There wasn't even a plane. One of the clouds looked like a rabbit. It was a little strange to think that up there somewhere an alien spacecraft was waiting to hear from my brother.

I checked my watch again. Three thirty-three. Almost countdown.

Three thirty-four. It was even stranger to think that my brother was counting on me.

I put my finger on the button. Three thirty-five. I started to count.

"... five ... four ... three ... two ... one ..."

I pushed.

Nothing happened.

I pushed again.

Nothing happened again.

What was wrong? Was I a second late? Had I broken it by carrying it in my book bag all day? I moaned out loud. My brother was going to kill me.

I shook the antenna. I pushed Play again and again.

And then something happened.

A voice behind me said, "Adam! Adam, what are you doing here?"

A voice behind me said, "Adam! Adam, what are you doing here?"

I spun around. There, right behind me, watching me, was Midge.

"What am I doing here?" I yelled. "Never mind what I'm doing here. What are *you* doing here?"

He pushed back his glasses. "Your father's birthday is in January," said Midge.

Chapter Eight

On the way home, I told Midge everything. Although I was worried about Keith's being able to read my thoughts, I decided that the risk was worth it. I really wanted to talk to someone about what was going on. And anyway, Keith needed *me* for a change. He was just going to have to lump it.

So I started at the beginning, when I got mad at Keith for not giving me a real present for my birthday. I told Midge about coming out to the park with Keith. And then I told him about Keith turning the lamp on and off without touching it and reading my mind.

Midge whistled. "Wow," he said. "That's pretty impressive." I knew he'd believe me. He peered over his glasses. "I always said Keith had to be from another planet, didn't I?" And it was true, he always had.

Finally I got to the end, when Midge had found me shaking the auxiliary antenna in a clump of bushes on the hill.

Midge said, "This is the auxiliary antenna? It looks like your brother's old Walkman."

"I know that's what it looks like," I said. "But you should've seen it yesterday, Midge, when I turned it on in our room. The lights really were going on and off, and there was all this noise . . . It was really weird . . . For a minute I thought the whole house was going to take off."

The next thing Midge said was, "I don't understand, Adam. Why don't you just let Them take your brother back to his planet? Think how much easier your life would be if Keith were in another galaxy."

"Plus I'd have my own room." I said.

"Plus you'd have your own room," Midge nodded. "And you wouldn't have to wait for hours just to get in the bathroom."

We came out of the park and wheeled our bikes to the left. "I'd let Them have him, if I were you," said Midge.

"I'm tempted," I said. "Don't think I'm not tempted."

And I was tempted. I'd been trying to imagine what it would be like, not having Keith around all the time. No one to nag me. No one to tease me.

No one to take my things without asking. No one to help himself to the last piece of cake or the last bar of chocolate. No one to hit me whenever he felt like it. No one to put itching powder in my socks or hide a chili pepper in Elvis's food. No

one to bother me every minute of the day and night (if you counted the number of times he'd woken me up screaming "Fire! Fire!").

I shrugged. "I don't know, Midge," I said. "I guess it's because he's my brother."

Midge wasn't the smartest boy in our class for nothing. "But he's not your brother," said Midge. "He's an extraterrestrial."

He had a point. "I know," I said, "but he's *my* extraterrestrial."

We crossed Zena Road.

"I guess it's like what you're always saying about you and your parents," I said. "They're not *really* your parents, because you're adopted, but now, in a way, they sort of are."

"Yeah," said Midge. "I see what you mean. But the thing is, Adam, I *like* my parents and they like me."

"I think my mom would miss him," I said. "She seems really fond of him."

We came to Prowse Avenue, where Midge would go one way and I'd go the other.

"Call me when you find out what happened," said Midge.

"I'll call you when I take Elvis for his walk," I promised. "I don't want Keith to hear me talking to you on the phone."

Midge shook his head. "I still think you should trade him in," he advised. "Maybe you'd get a better one."

Even though I couldn't see how the antenna's not working could possibly be my fault, I knew Keith was going to blame me. I mean, he always did, didn't he? He blamed me when Mom yelled at him. He blamed me when he didn't finish his homework. He blamed me when Dad gave him extra chores. Once he even blamed me because it was raining and his game was canceled. "It's your

74

fault, you little dork!" he'd yelled at me. "You're the one who said it was going to rain!"

I pedaled slowly down the road. If Keith hadn't managed to contact his ship, he was going to be furious. I was half expecting him to be waiting on the street so he could murder me without Mom hearing. But there was no one in sight.

I approached our house with caution. He wasn't waiting by the door or peeking out any of the windows. And I could just make out the sound of the radio coming from inside. That meant my mom was cooking. She always put the radio on when she was cooking. I felt pretty relieved. Everything was normal. Maybe Keith had gotten through to Them after all. He'd gotten through, and he wasn't going to be mad at me; he was going to thank me.

And then I came to a dead stop right in front of our gate. Everything wasn't normal. Elvis wasn't sitting in the front window. Elvis always sat in the front window, watching for me until I got home. He'd sit there all night if he had to. Keith said that was because Elvis was stupid. But my mom said it was because Elvis loved me.

And then this awful thought occurred to me. What if Keith did know that I'd told Midge? What if he'd done something to Elvis, the way he said he would?

75

For a few seconds I just stood there on the sidewalk staring at the empty front window. I could hear Keith saying, "You've got to promise, Adam. You've got to promise on the life of that mutt!" Elvis loved me and Keith had hurt him. *"Promise, Adam! Promise on the life of that mutt!"*

I was shouting as I burst through the front door. "Elvis!" I was yelling. I was practically crying, if you want to know the truth. "Elvis!" I dropped my bike in the hall and raced toward the kitchen. "I'll kill him!" I was yelling. "If he touched one hair on that dog's head, I'll kill him with my bare hands! I don't care where he comes from. I really mean it! I really, really will!"

I was so upset and in such a hurry that I guess I wasn't looking where I was going. One minute I was charging into the kitchen, and the next minute there was a howl of pain as I tripped over Elvis and flew across the room. I landed flat on my face in the middle of the kitchen floor.

"Have a nice trip?" asked Keith.

It took me about half a second to realize that he wasn't alone. Charlie was standing beside him. He lived down the street and was around a lot.

"Send us a postcard next time," said Charlie.

Then the two of them started laughing. I guess they'd been helping Mom set the table because they were both holding a bunch of silverware;

they were clutching each other and laughing so hard they could hardly stand up.

Elvis came over and licked my face.

My mother was at the stove. She was staring at me in disbelief. "Adam Wiggins," she said. She gave me a serious look. "Adam, what in the world's gotten into you?"

I didn't know how to answer that. Plus my knee was hurting. Plus Elvis was practically suffocating me. Plus Keith and Charlie had given up trying to stand and were doubled up on the floor, laughing

themselves sick. It was a really disgusting sight.

"Adam," said my mother. "Adam, I'm talking

to you. Just what do you think you're doing?"

"Me?" I said. How come she wasn't yelling at them? They were the ones who were making fools of themselves.

Keith managed to pull himself together enough to speak. "I told you he's crazy, Mom," he said. "I've been telling you that all along."

I'd been right. Of course Keith knew I'd told Midge. The first thing he said when we were alone in our room later was, "You told Midge, didn't you, Adam?"

I was still recovering from tripping over Elvis and everything, so I didn't even bother to lie. Not that it would have done me any good. You can't lie to someone who can read your mind, can you? So I collapsed on my bed and said, "Yes."

"Did you think I wouldn't find out, Adam?" asked Keith. "Did you think you could fool someone with my special powers?"

I tried to explain that Midge had followed me and caught me in the bushes with the auxiliary antenna, but Keith didn't want to listen.

He shook his head very slowly. "I knew I shouldn't have trusted you," he said. "You're unreliable, Adam. You can't be depended on."

"Yes, I can," I argued. "I can be depended

on. It wasn't my fault he followed me, was it? Do you think I told him to, Keith?"

But Keith was still shaking his head. "I don't want your excuses, Adam. I trusted you and you let me down."

"I didn't let you down," I protested. "I did exactly what you told me to do."

My brother made a face. "Did you?" he asked. "Then why didn't it work, Adam? How come I wasn't able to get in touch with my ship?"

"How do I know?" I yelled. "You're the one who —"

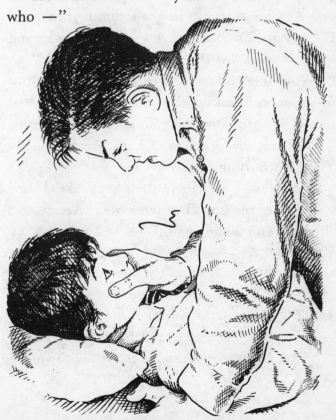

Keith clapped his hand over my mouth. "*Shhh,*" he hissed at me. "You want Mom to hear you? She already thinks you're losing your mind."

I tried to argue with this, too. "Mom doesn't think I'm losing my mind," I tried to mumble. "She just —"

Keith pushed me back on the bed. He lowered his face to mine. "Adam," said my brother, "I'm willing to give you one more chance. Do you understand? One more chance to prove to me that you can be trusted. One more chance to prove to me that you're not a dummy after all. But it's the last chance I'm ever going to let you have. If you blow this, that mutt is history."

"You won't be sorry, Keith," I promised. I'm no dummy. I had no idea what it was he wanted me to do, but I was already agreeing to do it. "You'll see how dependable I am. Really, Keith. You can count on me."

"I hope so," said Keith. "For your sake, I hope so." He let me up. "But remember, Adam, this chance won't come again."

Chapter Nine

I always take Elvis for a short walk before supper. So that was when I called Midge. Just in case my dad drove past or Keith left the house for something, I went to the next block and called him from the phone at the corner.

Only I had a hard time getting Elvis to sit still and be quiet. He kept knocking the change out of my hand because he was jumping around so much.

Midge answered on the first ring. "You're late," said Midge. "What happened? Didn't Keith get through to his ship?"

I had to hold Elvis's leash right near his head to hold him down. "No," I said, "he didn't get through."

"I knew it!" shouted Midge. "I knew it! I was really worried he'd done something to you when you didn't call sooner."

"That's because I had a little trouble getting through to you," I said. I glared at Elvis, but he was staring at the street. At least he had finally settled down. "Actually," I continued, "Keith wasn't as mad as I thought he'd be. He took it pretty well."

"Really?" said Midge. I was half expecting him to ask me *why* Keith took it so well, but instead he said, "That doesn't sound like your brother."

"I didn't say he wasn't mad at all, Midge," I explained. "And don't think he didn't blame me for the antenna not working, 'cause he did. But he definitely wasn't as mad as he could've been." I took a deep breath. "Not even about you."

"About me?" Midge's voice sort of squeaks when he gets excited. "I thought you weren't goint to tell him you told me."

"Calm down, Midge. I didn't tell him. He knew. Didn't I say he can read minds?"

Midge whistled. "Whew," he said. "That's pretty impressive." He whistled again. "And he wasn't pissed off?"

Elvis shifted a little. I gave his head a push.

"Not really," I answered.

Midge still didn't ask me why.

He lowered his voice. His mother must have come into the room. "So what happens now?" he whispered. "Does this mean he has to go back?"

He sounded hopeful.

"No," I said. "No, he's got another plan."

"Another plan?" asked Midge. "But I thought they were coming for him tomorrow. What's he going to do?"

"He isn't going to do anything," I said. "We're going to do it."

"We're going to do it," Midge repeated.

"Uh-huh." Just then Elvis spotted another dog. He stood up on his hind legs to get a better look. I pulled on his leash.

"And when are we going to do it?" Midge was asking.

"Tomorrow after school." I grunted. Elvis was straining to get free.

"Tomorrow after school," Midge repeated.

I felt that I was talking to an echo. What a week I was having. I'd just found out that my brother came from another planet. I was fighting with a dog who is almost as tall as I am when he stands up. And I was having a conversation with an echo.

"Uh, Adam," said Midge. He was talking very slowly. I could tell he was thinking. "Adam, just what is it we're going to do?"

Elvis started to bark and jump. The recorded voice asked me to deposit more money.

"Adam?" said the echo. "Adam, just what is it we're going to do?"

Elvis was going crazy. The line was about to go dead. It was going to be hard enough to explain Keith's plan to Midge without all this going on. "I'll tell you in the morning," I screamed. "First thing!"

"Adam!" Midge cried.

"Don't worry," I shouted as Elvis lunged free and the phone went dead. "You'll like it, Midge. It's going to be fun!"

"I don't like it," Midge grumbled. "I don't like it one bit." He bumped into a tree. He doesn't like to wear his glasses in the rain because they get wet and he can't see where he's going. But if he doesn't wear his glasses he can't see where he's going either. It's what my mother calls a dilemma. "Why can't he do it himself?"

I had a sudden urge to shove him into a puddle. I was feeling a little fed up. Not only was my arm getting tired from holding the umbrella over both of us, but Midge was being difficult. He gets like that sometimes. We were at school and he still hadn't agreed to help me with Keith's plan. "I've told you twice already," I said. "Keith thinks They'll take it better from us. If he tries to tell Them, They might just drag him into the spaceship and go."

Midge bumped into a garbage can. "I still don't think that's such a bad idea," he said angrily. "If you ask me, it's a lot better than your brother's idea."

Keith's idea was simple but awesome. The spaceship would be landing in the park that afternoon. The crew would be expecting Keith to be there so they could take him home. Only Keith wouldn't be there. Keith would be at 33 Chestnut Drive, locked in our room. Somebody else would meet the spaceship. Somebody else would explain to the crew that Keith was staying with the Wiggins family on a permanent basis.

Somebody else would give the captain of the spaceship the envelope containing the results of Keith's mission. Two somebody elses. Midge and me.

That was Keith's plan. Midge and I would go up to the park after school, and we would meet the spaceship when it landed. We'd explain to the captain that Keith had been trying to contact him but that his communicator had broken. We'd also explain that Keith had decided not to return to his planet, but to stay on Chestnut Drive with my parents and me.

"No, it isn't better," I said. We came to the corner and waited for the light to change. "Do you want me to tell you why it isn't better, Midge?"

The Walk sign flashed on. We started to cross.

Midge groaned. "No," he said, "you don't have to tell me. I knew there must be some reason Keith didn't get really mad yesterday. It was so we would do this for him, wasn't it?" Midge groaned again. "Because if we don't do what Keith wants he'll kill us, right?"

"Yeah," I said. "I think that's about right."

Midge splashed into a puddle. "But why me?" he whined. "I'm not his brother."

"No," I said, "that's true, you're not his brother. But you are my best friend. You can't let me meet with extraterrestrials by myself, Midge, can you?"

I switched the umbrella to my other hand. Midge and I changed sides.

"Oh, I don't know, Adam," said Midge. "I think maybe I could."

It's a good thing I knew he was kidding.

I decided to try a different tactic. "And anyway," I said, "you'd think you'd be at least a little excited about it. This is a real adventure. Think of it, Midge! You and I will be the first people on Earth ever to make contact with visitors from another planet! Don't you think that's pretty neat?"

"I think it would be a lot neater if it weren't raining," said Midge.

"The rain will stop by this afternoon," I assured him. "And even if it doesn't, Midge, don't you think meeting aliens is worth a little wetness? Can you imagine what the other kids will say when they find out?"

He looked over at me. Even though he was squinting, I could tell he was getting interested. "The other kids?"

"Not to mention the newspapers," I continued.

"The newspapers?"

"And television!" The umbrella trembled. I was pretty excited myself.

"Television?" He was squeaking.

"We'll be heroes, Midge. We'll be celebrities." I could see the flash bulbs popping and hear the crowds cheering. "It'll be like being an astronaut without having to leave the ground," I said. "Why, I bet we even meet the president!" I knew that would do it. Midge loves the first lady.

But he started shaking his head. "Wait a minute, Adam," he said as we turned down the road our school is on. School Street, it's called. "Don't you think you're getting a little carried away? We can't tell anyone about this. If we tell anyone, they'll find out about Keith."

"No, they won't," I said. I'd given this a lot of thought. "I mean, why should they? If we don't say anything, who's ever going to connect it with Keith? All we say is that we were taking a walk in the park and we just happened to find this spaceship and we talked to the guys inside it. Easy as pie."

We turned in at the school gate.

Midge grabbed hold of my arm. "Adam," he said. "Adam, hold on a second. I just thought of something else."

Boy, was he stubborn. My mom thought I was stubborn, but I was nothing next to Midge. "Come on, Midge," I pleaded. "I want to get inside."

But he wouldn't let go. "Adam," he said, "listen to me. This whole thing is crazy. They're not going to land a spaceship in the middle of the park on a Wednesday afternoon. Everyone will see Them!"

I smiled. I'd been saving the best part until last. "No they won't, Midge. Keith says the ship will be invisible."

"Invisible?" Midge repeated. "Adam, if it's invisible how will we know it's there?"

I smiled some more. "We'll know it's there, Midge, because we have something that will let us talk to the aliens and see the ship." I held up my book bag. "Right in here, Midge, I have Keith's communicator and his special glasses."

Midge whistled. "Whew, I'm impressed." He patted my shoulder. "I guess you've thought of everything," he said.

Chapter Ten

*B*ut I hadn't thought of everything. I'd forgotten Elvis. There was no way I was going to meet visitors from another planet without my dog. He'd protect me from anything.

So right after school, Midge and I raced over to my house. While we were there, he called his mother and told her he was going downtown with me, just to look around.

And I ran down to the basement, where my mother was lying on the ground, fixing the washing machine, and told her I was going downtown with Midge, just to look around.

Midge's mother said, "Don't be too late, Jerome. We're having your favorite for supper. Cauliflower with cheese."

My mother said, "In this weather?"

It hadn't exactly stopped raining.

"It's all right," I said. "We have the umbrella." And then I said, "Isn't Keith home yet?" I'd checked our room, where he was supposed to be hiding from the aliens, but he wasn't there. It was a little strange, because he should have been there by now. Keith's school is right around the corner from our house, so he can get home in just a few minutes.

"Of course not," said my mother. "He went over to Charlie's."

Charlie's? He was sending me and Midge on a mission of life and death and he'd gone over to Charlie's? What if we needed to get hold of him? And he said *I* wasn't dependable.

"Five o'clock," my mother called after me as I ran up the stairs. "Not a minute later, Adam, or it'll be bread and water for you tonight."

Midge and Elvis were waiting for me at the back door.

"Come on!" I cried. "Let the mission begin!"

"Have you lost your mind, Adam?" Midge yelled. "We can't sit under a tree! It's raining. What if it starts to thunder and lightning? We'll be killed."

I gave him a disgusted look. We'd walked miles to find this spot and I was exhausted. It's very tiring walking uphill in the mud, especially with a South Street retriever dragging you most of the way. And I was soaked. Water was seeping through my Windbreaker and my old green boots. The umbrella had blown inside out while we were still at the bottom of the hill. Even Elvis wasn't having a good time. He hates the rain. "Midge," I said, as calmly as I could. "Midge, if we don't stay under this tree there's a good chance we'll drown." I threw myself on the ground. Because it was under a tree, the ground was pretty dry, at least compared to every other inch of the park that we'd sloshed through. Elvis leaned against the tree.

Midge hunched down beside me. "I don't like this," said Midge. "There must be a better place where we can wait."

I pulled the map Keith had made me out of my book bag. It looked as if I'd pulled it out of the pond. I unfolded it carefully. I pointed to the spot Keith had marked with an *X*. "Look," I said, "see this? This is the tree we're sitting under."

"Yeah," said Midge, "I can see that's this tree."

I pointed a little in front of us. Just thirty yards away and a little to the left there was a slight dip in the hillside. "And that's where the ship's going to land," I said. "Right where it landed before."

"What time did he say They were coming?" asked Midge.

"Four o'clock, on the dot."

"They just better not be late," muttered Midge.

"Midge," I said, "these guys are a superior life form. They're not going to be late."

"What about the envelope?" asked Midge. "You didn't forget it, did you?"

He meant the envelope that had "Mission Results" printed in felt-tip pen across its front. I patted my chest. "Of course I didn't forget it. I have it under my shirt so it won't get wet." I reached into my book bag again. "Here," I said. "You take the sunglasses."

I handed them to Midge.

"You'd never know, would you?" said Midge. "They really look like ordinary sunglasses."

"They're very clever, these aliens," I shouted above the downpour.

"Oh my gosh!" screamed Midge. "I've gone completely blind."

I reached into my book bag one last time. "And I'll take the communicator."

He pushed the glasses up for a second. "It looks just like the antenna," he said.

"Don't you have any imagination?" I asked him. "Can't you see this one has a microphone built in? That's how he could fix it to transmit and receive."

"Okay, okay," said Midge. "I was only mentioning it."

Four o'clock came, but the spaceship didn't.

"I wish we'd thought to bring something to eat," Midge complained. "I'm starving."

"They won't be long," I reassured him. "Probably the weather's holding Them up."

Elvis had fallen asleep sitting up. I took my sweater out of my bag and put it over him.

At four-thirty, we changed equipment.

Midge put Keith's new Walkman under his jacket. I helped him adjust the headphones.

"How's that?" It wasn't easy getting his hood back on.

"Roger," said Midge. "Beam me up."

I put on the glasses. Everything went black.

"I really wish we had something to eat," said Midge.

I gave him a shove. "You're such a whiner, Midge. Why can't you just sit there quietly and do your job?"

"Because I'm hungry," Midge grumbled. "I'm hungry and my sneakers feel like fishbowls."

Elvis woke up. He looked around for a minute, like he wasn't sure where he was, and then he sort of cocked one ear.

"Look, Midge!" I said. "I think Elvis hears something."

"It's the rain," said Midge. "Or my stomach rumbling."

At five o'clock we changed equipment again.

"Right this minute, my mom's getting the cauliflower with cheese started," said Midge. "It'll be ready in half an hour."

It was hard to believe, but the rain seemed to be getting heavier.

I kicked him. Not hard or anything, just enough to make him shut up. It was bad enough that Elvis wouldn't stop whimpering without having to listen to Midge as well.

"And right this minute, my mom's getting a loaf of bread out for me," I told him. I shook myself, spraying the three of us. "She can forget about the water, that's for sure," I added.

By five-thirty, it was starting to be dark even without the sunglasses.

We swapped equipment again.

"Do you think They're really coming?" asked Midge. Now I could hear his stomach rumble.

"Of course They're coming," I said. "It's the storm."

But to tell the truth, I was beginning to have a few doubts.

I looked over at Midge, sitting all hunched up under the tree in the rain, wearing headphones under his Windbreaker hood. He looked like a jerk.

Midge turned to me. Even though it was hard for me to see, I could tell that he was thinking I looked like a jerk, too. A jerk sitting under a tree in the rain with a pair of sunglasses. A jerk, or one of Mrs. Vorha's turkeys.

Elvis was still sitting at the foot of the tree, whining. I was feeling a little bad that I'd taken him out of his nice dry house to sit in the rain.

"Ten more minutes," I said. "Then we go home."

"Okay," said Midge, trying not to sound too happy. "Ten more minutes."

*

Midge saw the lights first. Well, he would, wouldn't he? He wasn't wearing sunglasses.

"Adam!" he shouted. "Adam! What's that?"

"What?" I shouted back. "What's what?"

Midge pushed himself to his feet. "Don't you see them?" he squeaked. "The lights, Adam! Don't you see the lights?"

Elvis stood up too. His ears were up and he was staring in the direction Midge was pointing.

I threw the sunglasses down and stood up, too. Midge was pointing at the spot where the ship was supposed to land.

I shook my head. "What lights? I don't see any lights."

Midge kept pointing. "They were there, Adam. I swear they were. Two little beams of light. They looked like they were dancing."

Elvis kept barking.

"Dancing?" I asked. I looked at him closely. Maybe he'd caught a chill.

"Yeah, dancing." He grabbed hold of my arm. "There!" he screamed. "Look, Adam. There they are!"

I turned back to the landing area. There was nothing there but rain, and it was too dark now to really see that. "Midge," I said, "there's nothing there."

"Yes, there is," Midge insisted. "There are at

least two beams of light."

"Dancing," I said.

Elvis was throwing himself against the tree in a frenzy.

"Yes," yelled Midge. "Dancing." And then he punched me. "There, Adam! There they are!"

He was right! There they were. Two pale beams of light skipping through the rain. They reminded me of something, but I wasn't sure what.

Midge whistled. "Whew," he said. "That's pretty impressive, isn't it?"

I nodded. It was impressive, all right. But it wasn't exactly a spaceship. "It's not exactly a spaceship," I said.

Elvis was going crazy. I glanced over at him. He seemed to be trying to climb the tree.

Midge shrugged. "Maybe they're the spaceship's searchlights," he suggested.

That was what they reminded me of. Searchlight beams. "Yeah," I said, "that must be it. Searchlight beams. But where are they coming from?"

We both looked at Elvis clawing at the tree. Then I looked at Midge and Midge looked at me.

I could tell from his face that we'd both thought of the same thing at the same time. If they weren't searchlight beams, they were flashlight beams. And if they were flashlight beams . . . If they were flashlight beams, my brother probably wasn't far away.

"The envelope," whispered Midge. "Adam, check the envelope."

I dug under my Windbreaker and my shirt and pulled out the envelope. I ripped it open.

"Toilet paper!" we said together. "It's toilet paper!"

Midge looked at me and I looked at Midge. We both looked up.

"Keith Wiggins!" I shouted. "Keith Wiggins, get down from that tree!"

The spots of light began to dance over me and Midge.

Elvis started to howl.

"Roger!" yelled Keith. "Beam me up!"

"Look," screamed Charlie. "Look! The spaceships are dancing!"

The two of them started laughing and laughing.

"Where are your special glasses, Adam?" roared Keith. "Where are the glasses the smart aliens gave you?"

"Hand me my communicator!" gasped Charlie. "Quick! I want to transmit!"

"You just wait till I tell Mom!" I shouted. "You just wait."

They laughed so much they practically fell from the tree.

If they had, neither of us would've helped them up, I can tell you that.

My mother was shouting at us even before we got through the door. "What kind of time do you call this?" she was shouting. "You had me worried sick."

Keith was ahead of me. He was still laughing. He'd been laughing all the way home. I was sure he must've wet his pants, but you couldn't tell, we were so soaked anyway. "It's all right, Mom," he was saying. "I can explain everything."

Mom pointed behind her. "In!" she said. "Just get into the house." And then she saw Elvis and me. I guess we didn't look too good. "Adam," said my mother, "Adam, where have you been?"

I'd been all right until then. Even when I'd gone for Keith and he'd thrown me down. Even when Keith and Charlie had made fun of us all the way home. Even when Keith had told me how he'd set up the whole thing, right from the start. How he made the light blink by leaning on the bed because the outlet's right behind it. How he spied on me when I hid my birthday money so he could prove that he'd read my mind. And the second time, when he'd convinced me that his old Walkman was an antenna, Charlie had been under Keith's bed the whole time. Making the light go on and off. Making that hum. Making the static. They'd even hooked up the speakers to the new Walkman, one under his bed and one under mine, so that I wouldn't know where the sound was coming from. I'd been fine through all of it. But the minute I saw my mom I started to cry.

"Midge and I went to the park," I mumbled.

"In the rain?" asked my mother. Why did she always look at me like that? As if she couldn't believe her ears. "Why would you go to the park in the rain?"

"We went to meet the spaceship," I said.

"The spaceship?" said my mother. She looked very, very serious.

Keith started howling with laughter from the kitchen.

"Let me guess," said my mother. "Are we talking about Starship Keith Wiggins here, or what?"

My mom made me take a hot bath, and when I came out she had my supper waiting for me. It wasn't bread and water. It was macaroni and cheese. My dad went out for ice cream and he took me with him. He told me how his older brother had always played jokes on him when he was little, just like Keith. I didn't want to say, "Yes, Dad, I know. You always tell me that," so I just acted surprised. "Uncle Bill?" I asked. "But he's so nice."

"Keith's nice, too," said my dad. "It's just hard to tell sometimes."

And that night, when I went to bed, there was a package on my bed. It was a small brown bag with a white bow stuck to it.

"What's that?" I said to Keith. "Some sort of bomb?"

"'Course not," said Keith. "It's your birthday present."

"My present? But you gave me my present." To tell you the truth, I was a little afraid to open it.

"This is the real present," said Keith. "Go on, open it. It's not going to bite you."

I wasn't so sure about that. I opened it carefully and peered inside. It was small and flat, like a card.

"Go on," said Keith. "Take it out."

I took it out. It was the picture of Bo Jackson that used to be in Keith's key chain. At least it looked as though it was. Only it was signed. Actually, it was more than signed. It said: "To Adam, Best Wishes, Bo Jackson."

I looked at Keith. "Is this for real?" I asked him.

He acted all hurt. "Of course it's for real," he said.

I stared at the photograph. It looked real enough. It was written in ink and everything. "Where'd you get it?"

"What'd I tell you?" asked Keith. "Didn't I say I met him at the mall?"

"You mean you really did?" Keith had met Bo Jackson and asked him to sign his picture for me.

"Sure," said Keith. He winked. "You know I never lie to you."

DYAN SHELDON says, "This kid Adam just walked into my head and we went on from there. I stopped working on everything else and wrote the book. I really love Adam because, in spite of everything, he's so incredibly trusting." She is the author of several children's books, including *Harry and Chicken*, an *American Bookseller* Pick of the Lists title, and *Tall, Thin, and Blonde*. In addition to writing for children, Dyan Sheldon is an adult novelist and a humorist. She lives in Brooklyn, New York.

DEREK BRAZELL grew up in Canada and moved to London in 1980. He studied graphic design and illustration at Middlesex Polytechnic and since his graduation has worked in the fields of both advertising and children's book publishing.